For Fiona and Joe

With thanks to Mum for my own 'special tin'

Tricycle Press
P.O. Box 7123
Berkeley, California 94707
www.tenspeed.com

Library of Congress Cataloging-in-Publication Data

Inns, Christopher
Next, please! / Christopher Inns.
p. cm.
Summary: Doctor Hopper and Nurse Rex Barker treat their fellow stuffed
animals' ailments at the animal hospital.
ISBN 1-58246-038-8
[1. Toys—Fiction. 2. Hospitals—Fiction. 3. Medical care—Fiction.] I. Title.
PZ7.I5865 Ng 2001
[E]—dc21
00-036457
First printing, 2001
Printed in Hong Kong

1 2 3 4 5 6 7 — 05 04 03 02 01

NEXT!
Please

Christopher Inns

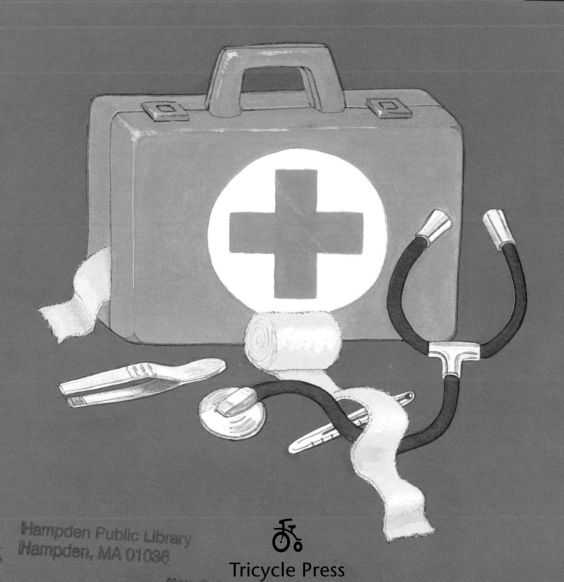

Tricycle Press
Berkeley / Toronto

Doctor Hopper works in a toy hospital.
It is her job to make sick toys better.

"Who is in the waiting room today, Rex?"

Today's Patients

1. One Eye Ted

2. Woolly Sheep

3. Wonderhorse

4. Sniffer the Dog

5. Sawdust Cat

Rex calls in a patient every time
Doctor Hopper shouts...

NEXT!
Please

One Eye Ted
first, Rex.

One Eye Ted's eye
has come off.

Doctor Hopper asks Rex
to fetch the special tin.

Hmm,
let me see.
Aha!

SPECIAL TIN

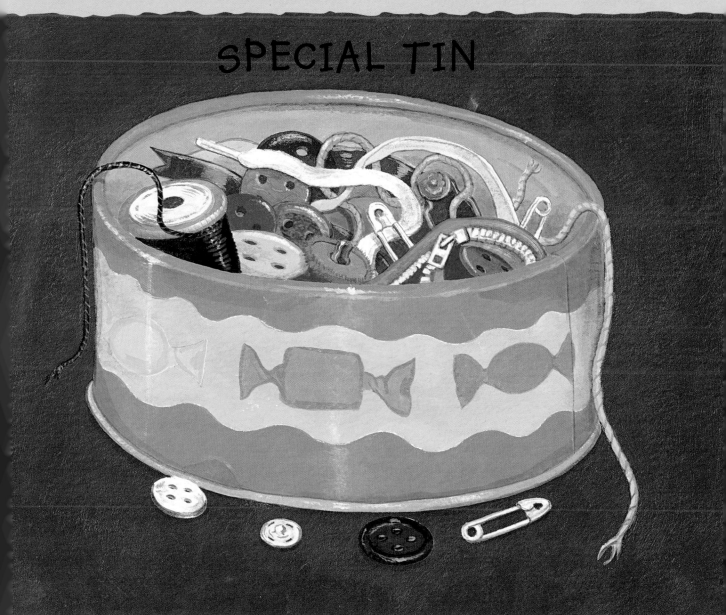

Doctor Hopper finds two new eyes and puts them on.

Now he will be called Two Eye Ted.
Doctor Hopper shouts...

It's Woolly Sheep.
She is becoming unstitched.

Doctor Hopper undoes the knots
and Rex gets knitting…

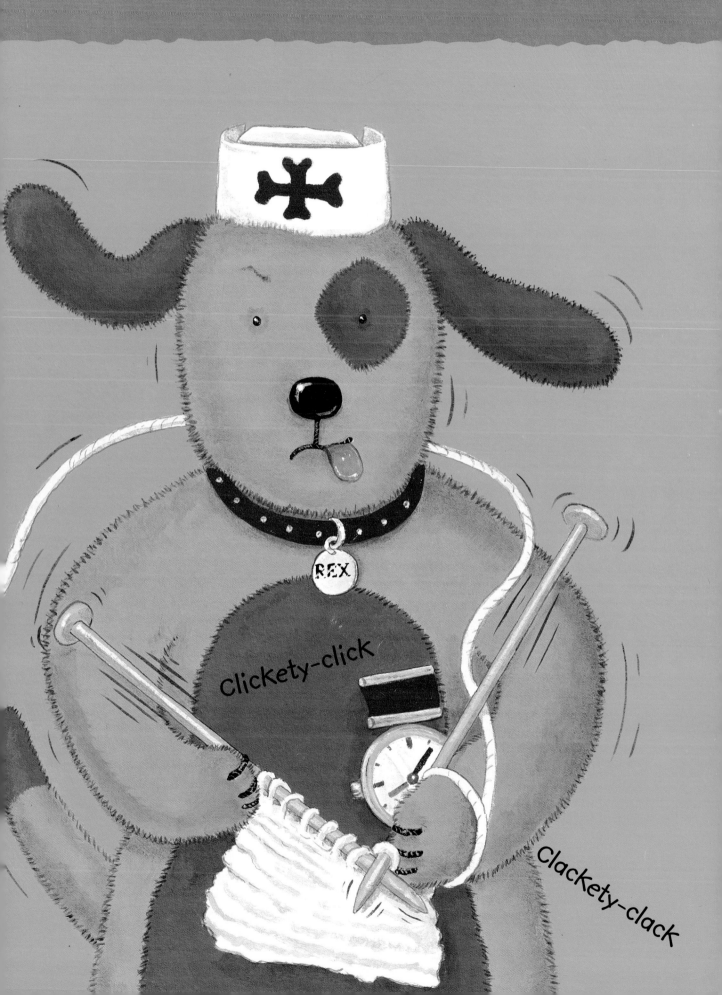

One of Wonderhorse's wheels
has fallen off.

Children cannot ride him if he does not roll along.

Rex holds Wonderhorse while Doctor Hopper fixes the wheel back on with something secret from the special tin.

Wonderhorse is very pleased.
He rolls as fast as when he was new.
Doctor Hopper shouts...

The next patient is Sniffer the Dog.
Sniffer doesn't have a nose.

Doctor Hopper sticks Sniffer's
nose back on.

Oops!

That's better.

Doctor Hopper shouts...

NEXT!
Please

Last on the list is Sawdust Cat.
She has bald patches from being
loved and cuddled so much.
She has lost her smile.

There is nothing Doctor Hopper can do.

But Rex thinks of something
to tell Sawdust Cat
to make her feel better.

Sawdust Cat thinks about this
for a while...

...and then smiles!

Doctor Hopper shouts ...

NEXT!
Please

But there is no one left in the waiting room. Doctor Hopper and Rex sit down and have a cup of tea and a cookie. They think about tomorrow and who will be...